For Hank, Joe, and Ellen

—M. I. B.

To Wade and Becky, who know a good parade when they see one

—K. H.

SIMON & SCHUSTER BOOKS FOR YOUNG READERS

An imprint of Simon & Schuster Children's Publishing Division ▸ 1230 Avenue of the

Americas, New York, New York 10020 ▸ Text copyright © 2010 by Michael Ian Black ▸ Illustrations copyright

© 2010 by Kevin Hawkes ▸ All rights reserved, including the right of reproduction in whole or in part in any form. ▸

SIMON & SCHUSTER BOOKS FOR YOUNG READERS is a trademark of Simon & Schuster, Inc. ▸ For information about special discounts

for bulk purchases, please contact Simon & Schuster Special Sales at 1-866-506-1949 or

business@simonandschuster.com. ▸ The Simon & Schuster Speakers Bureau can

bring authors to your live event. For more information or to book an event, contact

the Simon & Schuster Speakers Bureau at 1-866-248-3049 or visit our website at

www.simonspeakers.com. ▸ Book design by Dan Potash ▸ The text for this book is set in Claude Sans.

▸ The illustrations for this book are rendered in acrylics. ▸ Manufactured in China ▸ 0719 SCP ▸

11 ▸ Library of Congress Cataloging-in-Publication Data

▸ Black, Michael Ian. ▸ A pig parade is a terrible idea / Michael Ian Black ; illustrated by

Kevin Hawkes. ▸ p. cm. ▸ Summary:

Explains precisely why, although it may

sound like a good idea, gathering hundreds

of pigs to march in a parade through

one's hometown is inadvisable. ▸ ISBN 978-1-4169-7922-7

(hardcover : alk. paper) ▸ [1. Pigs—Fiction. 2. Parades—

Fiction. 3. Humorous stories.] I. Hawkes, Kevin, ill. II. Title.

▸ PZ7.B5292Pig 2010 ▸ [E]—dc22 ▸ 2008051562 ▸

A Pig Parade Is a Terrible Idea

Michael Ian Black

Illustrated by Kevin Hawkes

Simon & Schuster Books for Young Readers

NEW YORK   LONDON   TORONTO   SYDNEY

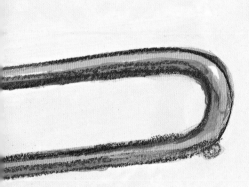

Like most children, you have probably thought to yourself at one time or another, *I bet a pig parade would be a lot of fun.* And yes, a pig parade certainly *sounds* like fun. It's even fun to say. Go ahead—say "pig parade" a couple times.

Fun, right?

After all, what could be more fun than gathering a few hundred pigs together for a grand parade, and then watching them proudly march together in perfect formation down the finest boulevard of your hometown?

The only problem is, a pig parade is a terrible idea.

For one thing, pigs *hate* to march. They prefer to snuffle, which is kind of like walking with your nose. Snuffling is fine when trying to find leftover apple skins and acorns around the barnyard. But snuffling is simply an inappropriate way to conduct yourself along a parade route.

That's just one reason why a pig parade is a terrible idea.

Also, pigs *absolutely refuse* to wear majorette uniforms. Even if you are able to find enough majorette uniforms for all of your pigs (which is a very difficult job in and of itself), just try getting those hundreds of pigs to put them on.

They will not do it.

Perhaps they
consider majorette
uniforms unflattering.

Nonsense.

Everybody looks sharp in a majorette
uniform, even pigs (*especially* pigs!). But
when you try explaining that to them, they
just look at you as if you are speaking a
language they do not understand.

Again, a pig parade is a terrible idea.

You cannot have a parade without floats, right?

Well, forget it. Pigs don't care about floats. Pigs don't care about all the time and energy you spent creating a "Three Little Pigs" float or a "Wilbur the Pig from *Charlotte's Web*" float. In fact, the only floats pigs care about are root beer floats, which they love.

Then there is the matter of music. Pigs have *horrible* taste in music! If you give a group of pigs marching-band instruments to play, do you think they will play good, spirited marching-band music?

No, they will not.

They will play sad, sad country music ballads with titles like "My Tears Are Wet 'Cause My Mud's Gone Dry" and "I Just Wanna Plop into This Bucket of Slop." That kind of music is fine for slow dancing at hoedowns, but it is *not* appropriate for a parade.

Face it, a pig parade is a terrible idea.

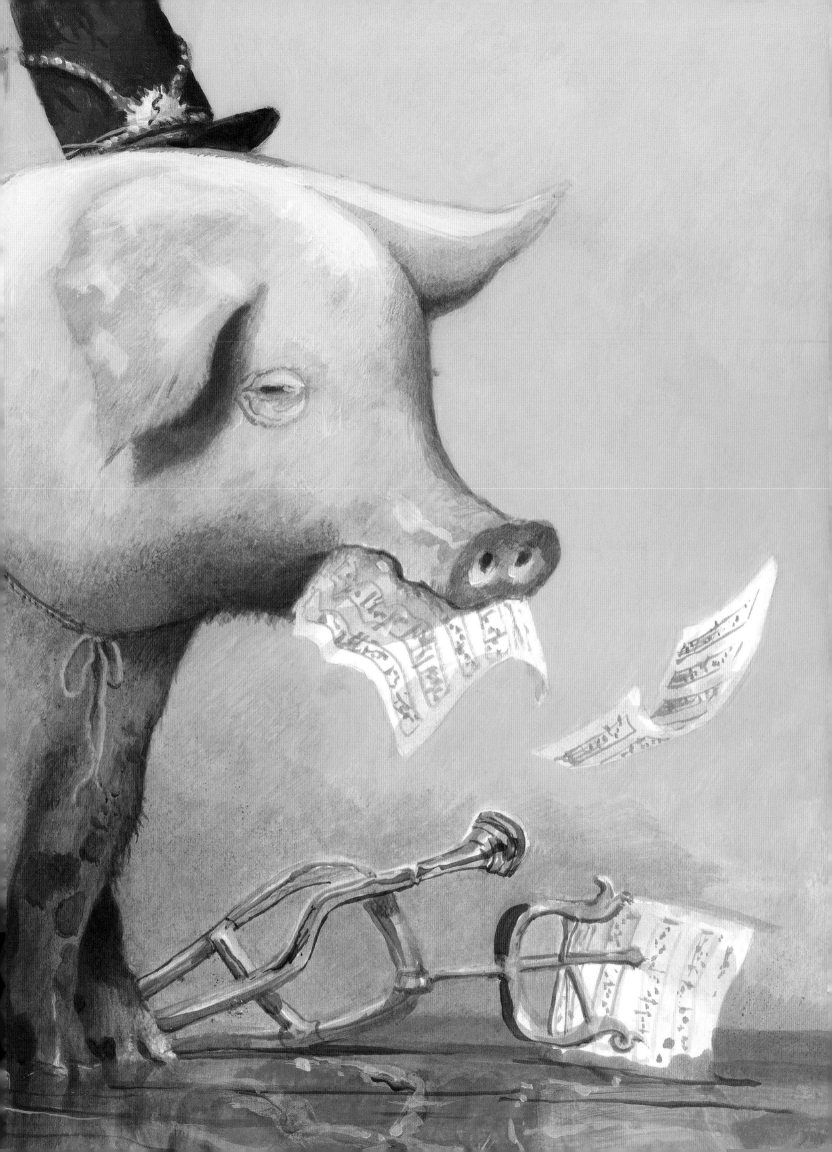

Finally, there are the giant balloons to consider. Everybody knows that giant balloons are the best part of any parade. Well, who do you think is going to hold all those balloons to keep them from flying away? The pigs, right? Wrong! Even if pigs *wanted* to hold the balloons instead of finding filthy puddles on the street to lie in, they couldn't do it. Because while pig hooves are good for digging up wild mushrooms, when it comes to holding giant parade balloons, they are simply not up to the job.

And what happens when balloons go unattended?

They bump into buildings or simply drift off into outer space, which would be fine for Martians but awful for those of us trying to enjoy a pig parade here on Earth.

So, when you consider the constant snuffling, the refusal to wear majorette uniforms, the disinterest in pig-themed literary floats, pigs' preference for weepy country ballads, and their utter lack of discipline regarding proper balloon handling, it should be absolutely, completely, and *totally* clear that a pig parade is a terrible idea.

A panda bear parade, on the other hand, would be fantastic!